THE STALKER'S OBSESSION

EMMA BRAY

Copyright © 2021 by Emma Bray

All rights reserved.

No part of this book may be reproduced in any form or by any electronic or mechanical means, including information storage and retrieval systems, without written permission from the author, except for the use of brief quotations in a book review.

Chapter One

Kylie

I rush along the busy sidewalk, excusing my way past strangers. I get more than one irritated look as I brush and bump past people, but damn it, I don't want to be late for work again.

Granted, I only work at the city library, but it's still a job, and it's one that I actually kind of like. I can't afford to go to college, so working at the library is the next best thing for a girl like me from the wrong side of the tracks.

I huff, irritated at myself. There's no good reason

for me to consistently run late every day. Hell, I live alone, but the problem is my over-zealous neighbor.

Mike has been trying to date me since day one I moved into the apartment building. I've repeatedly told him as nicely as I can I'm not ready for anything like that. That doesn't stop him from losing hope, though. Almost every morning now, he comes out of his apartment, which is unfortunately right across from mine, when he sees me leaving. He'll strike up the most ridiculous conversations, and me being the nice girl that I am struggles to break away as politely as I can.

I'm torn. Part of me wants to scream at him to fuck off, but the other part of me knows that I can't afford to make enemies in the building. This is the nicest apartment building I've ever lived in. I'm finally somewhat stable and not scraping for a place to stay or food to eat. I don't want to have to move again.

I hear my phone ringing and look down to dig in my purse, all the while never slowing up in my frantic move toward the huge three-story building that is the library. I'm almost there…

Just as I find my phone and pull it from my purse long enough to see my boss' name flashing on the screen, I collide into a brick wall—well, it feels like a brick wall anyway.

My arms flail up on instinct, my phone still clutched tightly in my hand. I know I'm going to fall, and I wonder how I could have veered off course so much that I ran into a wall.

I don't topple over as expected, though. Instead, I find myself steadied by strong hands. Huge hands that nearly wrap all the way around the tops of my arms where they hold me.

My eyes travel from the hands up decidedly masculine arms to a muscled chest covered with a black T-shirt, a strong, stubbled jawline and then stormy gray eyes regarding me more intensely than I think anyone has ever looked at me in my entire life. A lock of dark hair falls to the side of his forehead as he gazes down at me—and "down at me" is definitely the correct way to describe it. He's tall—at least a head taller than me, if not more—and big, like he works out all the time. His muscles are bulging underneath the sleeves of his short-sleeve shirt, but with that errant lock of hair falling into his eyes, I can't help thinking that he looks like a cross between a convict and one of the male models found on the covers of romance novels.

He's nothing but solid muscle, power radiating off of him.

It's a good thing his hands are still holding me up because I feel my knees go weak as his eyes pin me to the spot as if he's seeing deep inside me. It's insane, and I feel my body flush with embarrassment as if he's seen some secret part of me I've never shared with anyone. I know that's also a crazy reaction and wonder what's wrong with me. My nerves must be on edge by Mike and all his bullshit.

My phone is still ringing shrilly, the damn thing that caused all this, but I'm actually grateful for it now because it snaps me back to reality.

"I'm—I'm so sorry," I stammer as I get my wits back about me and pull back from him, breaking hold from his huge hands and piercing gray eyes that look like they're about to devour me.

I answer my phone and hurry the last few steps to the library, putting as much distance between me and the dangerously intense man as possible, while my boss yells at me on the other end of the line for being late—yet again.

<u>Chapter Two</u>

Liam

I'm watching the pretty blonde's long curls bounce just above the small of her back as she hurries away from me in a flurry like a butterfly that landed on me for just a moment before flitting away. Her lithe hips are swaying innocently, but what the sight's doing to me is anything but innocent. *Fuck*, I inwardly groan to myself.

I can't believe I'm standing in the middle of the sidewalk fighting a hard-on. When she ran into me with that soft, little body, I felt her pert tits smash up against my chest, but it wasn't that that did it. It was those huge blue eyes framed with thick lashes that sent an electric jolt through my system.

Something in their depths calls to me. They're like the ocean, and I fell into their abyss upon sight, drowning in them.

And her rosy little mouth opened in a perfect "o" that made me want to fill it with my cock…Christ Almighty.

Her little pink skirt is too short, barely covering her ass, and I'm wondering what the hell she's thinking leaving her house dressed like that. Her white button-up shirt provides enough coverage on the surface, but coupled with that little skirt flaring out around her hips, it's sinfully innocent, which doesn't make a damn bit of sense.

I shake my head. What the hell's wrong with me? It's obviously been too long since I've gotten laid.

Not that I have a problem getting women. I know I can have any woman I want. Not being cocky. Those are just facts. The fact that I'm a billionaire certainly doesn't hurt anything, though my billionaire status isn't anything I ever chased. The business was passed down to me by a stubborn father who wanted his son to follow in the family business. No matter that I didn't give a flying fuck about being a businessman. And I still don't. The old man would be turning over in his grave if he knew I let others run the corporation and simply benefited from the monetary gain.

Money talks, especially with the opposite sex. The simple fact is I'm tired of the charade, the endless women whose faces all blur into one. I don't even have to buy them dinner to get in their pants. All I have to do is drive up in my Ferrari or Bugatti and they're more than willing. It's…tiresome.

I long ago started relieving myself with my trusty fist. It's just easier. Besides, after my time in the marines, I value my privacy. I live alone, and that's the way I want it. People get on my damn nerves. I only come out for a run every now and then, like I'm doing today, to get some fresh air. And because physical training is just ingrained in me. I stay fit, making sure I'll always be a weapon of mass destruction if need be. I've done my time in the military and got honorably discharged when my old man passed, leaving everything to me. I guess I should have made a career of it with my willpower. That ship hasn't totally sailed yet. I can always rejoin, and I've thought of it a time or two.

It's the privacy issue, though. I don't savvy the thought of being packed into a bunker with ten other fuckers like a can of sardines.

Naw, I'm over that shit.

It's pitiful really. I have all the money in the world. I can go anywhere I want and do anything I want, but I'm bored with all of it. Bored with life.

Until now…

I continue to watch my little butterfly as I suddenly realize in a moment of clarity that she's exactly what I've been waiting for.

It's crazy, and I know it. I also know I'm not the crazy type. I haven't gotten where I am today by making rash decisions. Maybe I've finally and truly lost it, but something about her has drawn out the beast in me. Like a wolf imprinting on his mate, our eyes clashed, and now I feel like my life will forever be entwined with hers.

I don't know anything about her. But something tells me she's different.

All I know is that I want her. I want her more than I've ever wanted anything in my entire life. And asshole that I am, I always get what I want.

She flits up the stairs to the library, and I'll be damned if I don't move to follow her.

Chapter Three

Kylie

Unlike a lot of people, I actually enjoy my job. I'm not one of those who can't wait to get home. I was never considered the nerdy type in school, but books are my friends. After my parents died, I threw myself into reading to keep my thoughts from turning to self-pity. I also didn't want to be a bother to an aunt and uncle who had only taken me in out of a sense of obligation. I tried to be as quiet as possible so they wouldn't even know I was there. It must have worked too because they were able to go on about their lives like I didn't even exist.

Oh, they weren't cruel to me. They made sure I had food and clothing. They were like cordial strangers. Polite and aloof. I stayed with them for two years—just until I turned eighteen. Once I reached the age of maturity and they weren't legally responsible for me, I politely thanked them for their charity and hit the road. They wished me the best, but there wasn't an extended invitation offered, and I'd seen the relief in their eyes to have their duty discharged.

I haven't seen them since. There are no parental phone calls checking up on me. I'm on my own now.

I guess I can't blame them. They didn't sign up to raise a kid. My parents did that, and then they went and died in a car crash, leaving me behind.

Anyway, I discovered a love for reading—one I had to lay to the side when I first struck out into the world on my own. I literally left my aunt and uncle's place with nothing but the clothes on my back and a small suitcase.

I worked several shitty jobs at the local temp agency, making just enough in one day to pay for one night at a barely decent motel so I wasn't out on the streets.

Finally, a permanent position became available here at the library, and I pounced on it. It's like fate was finally smiling down on me because how perfect was it for a book lover like me to get to work around the tomes I'd fallen in love with?

Shortly after I got that big break, I got another one in the form of an apartment vacancy posted on one of the community bulletin boards at the library. I know it was wrong, but as soon as it was posted and I saw it, I yanked the ad down so no one else could nab it out from under me and ran over to the apartment building I now live in to put my name in the hat. Miracle of miracles, I got it.

It's not the Ritz-Carlton or anything, and no doubt many people would turn their noses up at it. It's not in the best part of town, but it's not in the worst either. Maybe the paint is peeling just a little bit on the frame of the doorway. But it's all mine.

I'm taking care of myself. I'm surviving with no parents, and I'm not a burden to anyone.

I'm so grateful for this job, and this library is like home to me. Plus, on my breaks, I can read about all the amazing places I know I'll never be able to afford to visit.

I know it's such a cliche, but I really want to go to Paris. I want to see the Eiffel Tower and the Paris Opera House. Those are at the top of my list.

I also want to visit England, Scotland, Ireland, Italy, Greece, and countless others. There are so many beautiful places out there that aren't meant for an orphan like me.

I can't keep my concentration on what I'm reading today, though. I read the same sentence again for at least the tenth time, but a pair of fierce gray eyes keep clouding my vision.

I snap the book shut and groan in frustration. I close my eyes, and still those stormy gray eyes are there. I can't escape them.

I don't know what it is about them that haunts me so. They were beautiful, no doubt, a color unlike any I've ever seen before. Smoky, the color of the moon or a wolf's hide.

Wolfish. A shiver runs up my spine at the thought, though it's not one of fear. I'm not sure what this odd feeling is exactly. Anyway, wolfish. That's what his gaze was like. Animalistic. Predatory. I tremble at the memory, my body feeling flushed.

I remember how large he was. He'd towered over me dangerously, but his hands had felt gentle on my arms. I let my mind wander to what it would feel like to have his arms wrapped around me. What it would be like to brush that lock of dark hair back from his head. It looked silky, like a raven's wing.

What would his kiss be like?

Although I'm nineteen, I'm still a virgin. I only

dated a couple of times in high school, and I've never done much more than kissing. Somehow I don't think *his* kisses would be like the fumbling ones of high school boys. I don't know what they'd be like exactly, but I guess the kisses of a man such as him would be something else entirely.

I blush when someone walks up to the desk to check out a book, making their presence known with a slight throat clearing. I know they can't possibly know what I've been daydreaming of, but my face still turns pink at the thought of being caught with my naughty thoughts.

Get it together, Kylie, I tell myself. *You don't even know this guy. He could be a serial killer for all you know. Or married. Or any number of things.*

I must be deranged to be thinking like this. To be fantasizing over a total stranger. Someone who I'm sure I'll never see again.

Maybe the loneliness is getting to me. I've always told myself I don't need anyone, that I like being alone, but my overactive imagination is proof that maybe I do need to get out more.

Chapter Four

Liam

I feel like such a creep, but I can't help it. I've been watching her for days now. She's like some mesmerizing creature I can't get enough of.

I have my driver drop me off every morning in that same area so I can watch my little butterfly as she flits to work. She's always flitting around erratically. Of course, that's because she's late almost every morning.

My jaw clenches and my hands fist at my sides as I stand on the other side of the street and contemplate a thousand ways to kill the bastard who keeps holding her up. The dumb ass prick who lives too close to her for my liking. I see the way he leers at her, and I know the depraved thoughts he's having. It takes every ounce of strength in me to not scoop my butterfly out of his path every morning—put her in a little jar where I can keep her safe—and beat him senseless for even daring to look at her.

I don't do it, though, knowing it would only frighten her to find out I've been following her. I'm not some sick pervert, I tell myself. I'm doing it to protect her. She's such a frail little thing. Anyone could crush her wings. If I'm there in the shadows, I can watch over her and make sure she's okay and that nobody harms her.

She's mine. I know it deep down inside. I've become obsessed with her, but I'm beyond caring. I've utilized my resources to their full extent to find out everything I can about her.

Kylie. Nineteen. Orphaned at sixteen. Graduated from high school at the top of her class. Not in college, though certainly smart enough to be. No husband or boyfriend, thank God. I don't know how I'd handle that. Just the thought of another man's hands on her makes the beast within me churn with jealousy.

I wonder if she's a virgin. Something about the

innocence in her eyes makes me think she is. My pulse thunders at the thought, and I feel my cock stiffening. The thought that she's never been with another man, that she could truly be mine, all mine, makes me want to race across the street, sling her over my shoulder, take her home with me and claim her with all the pent-up lust and love I feel.

Insanity. I know it's insane to feel this way over one look. How the fuck I could love her without having spoken two words with her is beyond me, but I know deep in my soul that I do and that I'd die to have her and protect her.

I haven't jacked off once since that fateful crash of our bodies. Oh, I want to. I need to. But I'm determined I won't come again until it's for her.

I need to introduce myself to her instead of stalking her like a hunter studying his prey, but I'm waiting for the right moment so she doesn't try to flit from my grasp again.

Maybe I'll walk into the library and ask for help finding a book. Maybe I'll casually run into her at the grocery store. I don't know how it's going to happen. I don't know when it's going to happen. But I know it's going to happen soon.

And I also know that whether she knows it or not, she belongs to me.

Chapter Five

Kylie

I feel a tingle at the nape of my neck and shiver, crossing my arms about myself and glancing over my shoulder. I've been feeling off all week—ever since I bumped into him, whoever he is.

I wish I could shake the feeling. I don't know what it was about the guy. He was a hunk, for sure, but I'm not the kind of girl who drools over hot guys—not that that's what I'm doing when my thoughts keep drifting back to him. It's not. That's ridiculous. And I'm smarter than that. I'm level-headed.

I am.

It was his eyes. They keep coming unbidden into my thoughts. I keep thinking back on their intensity and wonder what it means.

"Hey, gorgeous," Mike greets me as I round the corner of the apartment building.

I fight to keep from rolling my eyes. It's not enough that he accosts me every morning and makes me late for work. Now, it looks like he's going to start in on my evenings too.

"Hey, Mike," I try to be cordial but distant. I don't want to encourage him. Mike's not a bad-looking guy. I'm just not interested.

"Wanna grab a bite?" he asks hopefully.

I shake my head. "No, thanks." His smile falters.

"Long day at work," I add with a tiny smile to try to soften the blow. I really don't want any hard feelings with neighbors. This guy is relentless, though. You think he'd get the hint and stop asking already.

"Oh, come on, Kylie. We're neighbors." He leans over me with one hand braced against the brick wall he's somehow cornered me against, and an alarm bell starts to go off in my head.

His other hand comes up to grip my upper arm. Exactly where the man with the gray eyes gripped me to steady me. The difference is I hadn't been scared when the gray-eyed man gripped me there. The way

Mike grips me and the way he's looking down at me with something in his eyes I can't quite identify but know I don't like makes me very uncomfortable. I smell the alcohol on his breath as he dips his head down to lean even closer to me saying, "I can help you unwind."

"No, thanks," I say, trying to pull my arm away from him, but his grip tightens painfully, and he has me caged in against the brick wall with his other arm.

I feel the panic beginning to rise within me as his eyes darken. I don't know if it's the alcohol or if this is the real Mike coming out, but I just want to get as far away from him as possible.

"Mike, please let go of me," I try to say firmly, but my voice comes out shaky even to my own ears.

He grins and leers down at me before stepping forward and pinning me against the brick with his heavy body.

I feel something hard near his thighs pressing into me. Oh my god, does he have a gun? My heart is beating a thousand miles a minute.

When he rubs that hard thing up and down against me, a glassy look taking over his eyes, I suddenly realize with horror what it is and feel like I'm going to vomit. Both his hands grip my arms now, and I choke out, "Mike, stop! Please!"

I think my fear only turns him on even more because he presses harder into me. The streetlamp illuminates his steely eyes and hard mouth that's coming down to mine.

I turn my head from his impending kiss and begin to kick as hard as I can with my arms pinned down.

He only laughs, saying, "Man, you really know how to turn a guy on, Kylie," as he reaches for his zipper, and my panic goes full-fledged.

Oh god. Is he really going to rape me here right outside the back of our apartment building? My eyes try to glance frantically behind us, but it's dark outside the light of the streetlamp, and I know in the secluded corner of the apartment building where we live no one's home from their late jobs yet. Still, I try to scream, and his hand goes over my mouth while his other is still fumbling with his pants.

Suddenly I hear a growl, and Mike's wrenched off of me. I hear a bone-cracking thud and watch in a mixture of relief and shock as a fist connects with Mike's nose, laying him out flat on the cold concrete.

I look up to see the identity of my rescuer and am met with a pair of smoky gray eyes. *Those* smoky gray eyes. The ones that have been haunting me since that day on the street.

He came. He's here. How is he here? How is that

possible? My head hurts with the thoughts swirling inside it. I don't understand anything.

Mike doesn't move. The stranger with the gray eyes knocked him out with one punch. I watch the gray-eyed man's muscles bunch and cord as he flexes the hand he landed his punch with, those stormy eyes settling on me.

I feel my knees beginning to buckle as the gravity of what would have happened to me if he hadn't shown up when he did like some sort of god-like avenging angel hits me.

But where did he come from?

Chapter Six

Liam

I knew it. I knew I couldn't let her out of my sight for one moment. I got held up for just a minute—one minute because of damn, fucking people—trying to cross the street without getting too close to her and drawing unnecessary attention to myself. I hadn't wanted her to catch me following her, but damn it, that one moment is all it took to see my fears materialize. I'd exploded in a blind fury when I'd heard her strangled scream and seen that trash with his hands on her. My sweet little butterfly.

I reach for her as I see her starting to slide down the brick wall, the shock setting in. I steady her just like I did that first day on the street with my hands on her upper arms as firmly yet as gently as possible. My blood is still pumping fast within me, the adrenaline still racing through me. She was almost hurt. Fuck, I want to protect her so bad everything within me is crying out for me to pull her to my chest and hold her.

Judging by how she looks like she might faint that probably wouldn't be a comfort right now. It might scare her even more.

"I've got you," I tell her, fighting every instinct within me and making myself simply hold her up with my hands instead of gathering her into my arms. *Yes, I've got you, and I don't think I'm ever going to be able to let you go.* I can't stop the wave of possessiveness that washes over me when I look at her. Goddamn.

Her blue eyes shimmer in the light of the street-lamp, the golden highlights in her hair set off by the amber glow.

"Who—who are you?" she stammers hesitantly, her eyes wide.

"Liam." I answer her, trying to keep my voice even so as not to frighten her further.

"Liam," she repeats, her voice little more than a whisper. My eyes are pinned to her mouth and the way her little tongue shoots out to pronounce the "l" in my name. The way she says my name is like a punch to my gut, her voice so tiny and soft and sexy. Fuck. I want to hear her screaming it in that hot, little voice of hers while I ram my cock inside what I already know will be a tight pussy.

Jesus, what the fuck is wrong with me? She was attacked, and all I can do is think about fucking her. But I don't just want to fuck her. I want to stroke all her pain away. I want to give her my come like an offering from my body to hers, and then I want to hold her in my arms and worship her like the little goddess she is.

"I'm Kylie," she tells me shyly. I already know it. *Your name is Kylie Rena Johnson*, I want to tell her. *Rena is pronounced Renee. Your mother spelled your middle name like that when she was doped up on painkillers in the hospital after having you via cesarean section. People have been mispro-nouncing it as "ree-na" all your life.*

But I don't say any of that. I don't say anything. I just stare at her, drinking her up. Her pert little nose. Those luscious lips. And those eyes—those fucking eyes I could drown in.

Her cheeks turn a charming shade of pink under my perusal, and she asks me, "Where did you come from?"

I don't answer her because I don't want to lie to her, but I also don't want her to know I've been stalking her, especially considering what just happened to her. "Are you okay?" I ask her instead.

Hell, of course she's not okay. Her eyes fill with tears, and she tries to blink them away, my brave little butterfly, while she glances at the piece of shit still knocked out cold on the ground. Anger surges within me anew at how I'd found him on her. He doesn't know it yet, but he's just signed his death warrant.

"I..." she begins, looking around helplessly before shivering and continuing, "I can't stay here."

I'm glad she said it because there's no fucking way I'm going to leave her here alone.

"Come on," I say, releasing her arms to step back from her and hold a hand out to her.

I watch her hesitate for a moment before her eyes look up to meet mine. For a moment, I'm afraid she's going to refuse me, but she finally puts her tiny hand in mine trustingly, and my entire body registers the touch like an electric jolt.

I begin leading her toward the street while I speed

dial my driver with my free hand. She's going home with me where I can take care of her.

I'm still kicking myself that she came close to being hurt on my watch.

Nothing, *nothing*, like this will ever happen to her again. I guaran-fucking-tee it.

Chapter Seven

Kylie

The gray-eyed man—Liam—spoke to someone on the phone. It's hard for me not to think of him as the gray-eyed stranger. That's what I've been thinking of him as in my head for so long now.

"Everything's going to be okay now." He smiles down at me reassuringly. Now he's helping me into the back of a limousine. Holy cow. A limousine. I had to close my mouth to keep from gaping when it pulled up alongside us.

As if this night couldn't get any more bizarre. First, I'm assaulted. Then, I'm rescued by the stormy-eyed man. Now, he's guiding me into a limousine. Once again I find myself wondering who is this guy?

That's not the question I choose to ask, though, as he gets in behind me and sits across from me.

I notice again how huge he is. I can see the outline of his taut muscles underneath his black shirt. His legs seem to take up the whole space. My God, does he live at the gym?

I lick my lips, a nervous habit I've never been able to break. His eyes zone in on them like a hawk, and his breathing seems to hitch.

My heart speeds up within me, but I force myself to ask him, "Where are we going?"

"Somewhere safe," he answers simply, his eyes never straying from me. I simply nod in acceptance, not knowing what to say. The way he stares at me so intensely causes my own breath to hitch.

I must be crazy. I'm in a limousine with a guy I hardly—no, don't—know, and I'm letting him take me to an undisclosed location. What if I've just jumped out of the frying pan into the fire? From one deranged man to another?

But this one doesn't mean to hurt me. Does he? Why would he save me and hold me so gently if he means me harm? That doesn't make sense, right?

My thoughts must betray me on my face—my

dad always used to say my face was like an open book, that I couldn't hide anything—because Liam suddenly speaks again, softly yet intensely, "Don't be afraid, Kylie."

I look at him sitting across from me and strangely, I'm suddenly not afraid. Somehow I know this man won't hurt me. And God…the way he says my name, like he's caressing it with his tongue.

I feel a strange, pulsing sensation at the apex of my thighs, so I cross my legs to try to ease the ache.

His eyes finally leave mine to move to the flesh my movement has exposed. My skirt hikes up higher on my thighs as I cross my legs, and his breathing becomes ragged. His fists clench at his sides and for some reason, that coupled with his uneven breathing does something to my insides. I feel my tummy do a flip-flop.

I'm not entirely sure what's happening. I have almost zero experience with men, but I know I've never felt anything like this before. This feeling of electricity that both excites and confuses me.

Still tentatively looking at this huge man sitting across from me with his fists clenched as if he's barely restraining himself from something, I can't help but wonder what I've gotten myself into.

Chapter Eight

Liam

Her face blushes prettily under my gaze, and I know I should stop staring at her, but I can't. I can't believe I've finally got her here with me after watching her from afar for so long.

She's perfect. Even more perfect up close like this. When she crossed her legs, I got a glimpse of her lacy white panties, almost making me blow my load in my pants on the spot. Fuck, does she know what she's doing to me? One look into her tentative, innocent eyes and I know she doesn't, and fuck me, if that doesn't turn me on even more.

There's no doubt about it. I'm going to hell. The things I want to do to this innocent angel. There's probably a special cell down there with my name on it being prepared for me right now.

My cock is straining underneath my jeans, and now I'm treated to the sight of that pink skirt riding up higher on her thighs. Her beautiful legs are shapely and seem to go on forever.

Hell, I don't know how she can't see my cock bulging through my jeans, but she's so innocent and nervous, she's not even looking there. I wonder if she's ever seen a man's cock before, and I stiffen painfully even more at the thought that I could be her first.

"I'm sorry," she finally says.

My eyes snap back to hers. Maybe I was wrong? Maybe she's more aware than she lets on.

Once again, I curse myself. I'm such a bastard. Here she is fresh from being assaulted and all I can do is ogle her and think about fucking her when I should be trying to soothe her fears and make her feel safe. I mentally will my swollen member to subside. Of course, it rarely listens to me. My jaw clenches and hot anger surges through me again when I think back on that fucker's paws on her.

When I don't say anything, she continues, as if

trying to explain, "You're the man I bumped into on the street. I didn't mean to run into you like that. I was running late for work and wasn't paying attention to where I was going." Her face colors again, and she pulls nervously at the hem of her skirt.

I feel a rush of pleasure that she remembers me. I wasn't sure if she would. But I can't believe *that's* what she's sorry for.

"You might not remember," she adds, her fingers twisting in her lap

I give a course laugh, and she eyes me skeptically.

"Oh, honey, I remember." Fuck did I ever. That moment changed my life. I haven't thought of anything but her since.

Of course, she has no idea how blue my balls are just sitting in the same vicinity with her, smelling the flowery scent of her perfume, looking at her tight little body sitting right across from me. How long I've dreamed of this moment, of being this close to her.

It's obvious she needs reassurance from me that I don't hold that little collision against her. If she only knew I thanked God for it every night. For bringing her into my life. "I'm just glad I was there to keep you from falling," I tell her. *I'll always be there to keep you from falling. I'll save you from anything.*

She gives me a shy smile that does pitiful things to

my heart. I am so fucked. This tiny, fragile, little butterfly can grant me just the tiniest of smiles, and my chest clenches painfully. Why does she have this effect on me?

"Thank you." She's so polite, and damn it if that doesn't turn me on too. Hell, everything about her turns me on. "And thanks for saving me tonight too," she looks down. "I don't...I don't even want to think of...of what could have..." she stumbles over the words, and I can't help it. I reach out and place a finger over her quivering lips. *Damn it*. They're soft as rose petals.

Her blue pools shine up at me with unshed tears, and it's like an arrow has pierced my heart.

"No one's ever going to hurt you again," I tell her.

I've never meant anything more.

Chapter Nine

Kylie

My heart tripped within me when he called me "honey." I know it's a common moniker that lots of people use and that it doesn't necessarily mean it's a term of endearment, but I like him calling me it.

What's more is I believe him when he tells me he won't let anyone ever hurt me again. His words flow into me like a balm to my soul, and I relax. His finger is still on my lips as my mouth falls open softly in a gasp.

His gray eyes go stormy again, and he pulls his finger back with a curse.

I sit there unsure of what to do or say. I don't know what he expects of me—if anything. But then the limo comes to a stop, and he's stepping out before reaching a hand back inside to guide me out.

Again, I place my hand in his, but this time I have no hesitation. On the surface, this man is so much bigger, stronger, and scarier than Mike, but somehow I know he won't hurt me.

It's been raining, and even though I'm wearing flats, their bottoms are slick, so I slip on the pavement as I step out of the limo, crashing into his chest once again.

His arms wrap around me to keep me from falling, and then in a movement so swift it surprises me, he bends over and scoops me into his arms.

I gasp—both at his movement and when I see the enormous mansion we've pulled up to—and my arms instinctively go around his neck.

His eyes bore down into mine, and then they fasten onto my lips when I lick them again nervously. His eyes flash with something I can't identify but that causes my own pulse to race before he looks ahead and pulls me closer to his chest as he starts to walk up the steps leading to the massive doorway.

"It's slippery out here when it's wet," he tells me.

"Easier to just carry you than chance you falling and breaking that pretty little neck."

My cheeks heat with pleasure. Did he just call me pretty? I chance a peek at him. He thinks I'm pretty? The thought that he thinks so makes me smile inside.

I know he's only carrying me for practical purposes, but I can't help but savor being carried by this man. I blush when I remember wondering what his arms would feel like. Well, now I know, and it's so much better than I could have imagined. I feel his hard pecs through his shirt, and his arms are like steel around me. I feel so tiny in his arms, and he carries me effortlessly. I feel…safe.

Chapter Ten

Liam

I'm painfully aware of every inch of her body that's pressed up against me, and fuck, she feels good. Her tiny arms are wrapped around my neck, and I can't help but imagine them wrapping around my neck like this with me on top of her claiming her for all that's in me.

I cross the threshold, and then I see her look up at me, her eyes wide and innocent, regarding me as if I'm a hero.

I can't stop the groan that escapes me. "You're going to have to stop looking at me like that, honey," I tell her.

Her little brow furrows. "Like what?"

She honestly doesn't know. I set her on the ground, but I can't help letting her body slide down mine on the way down. Fuck it all. Her body feels too good against mine.

"Nevermind," I growl. Her long, golden hair falls over her shoulders and down her back. It brushes my arms and hands as I hold her waist. She's so fucking sweet and beautiful. A tiny little slip of a thing with this gorgeous mane of luscious locks. I can hardly stand it.

"Why are you being so nice to me?" she whispers up at me. She's serious. She really doesn't understand.

"Why wouldn't anyone be nice to you?" I ask her just as seriously.

She shrugs, a tiny, sensual lift of her shoulders that's made even more alluring just knowing that she doesn't know what she's doing. She has no idea how sexy she is, how each movement she makes is like that of a goddess.

"You just came out of nowhere, like a guardian angel," she continues softly before looking up at me in awe.

I laugh sardonically at that. "I'm no angel, baby." God, if she only knew the thoughts I've had about deflowering her.

When she shakes her head, disagreeing with me

and looking up at me so trustingly, my throat tightens, and I'm humbled by the faith and admiration in her eyes. I'm also shamed by it. Would she feel the same way if she knew I've been secretly watching her ever since that fateful day we collided?

"I can't believe our paths crossed twice," she comments. "First, I run into you, and then you're saving me. Well, you saved me both times, really." She smiles up at me shyly again, and I want to cut my heart out and hand it to her on a silver platter. I want to die for her to prove my love to her. I'd cut my hand off if she told me to. I want to save her from anything and everything that would ever harm her or make her cry. She has no idea what I'd do for her.

I know now's not the time to tell her all that, though. She's still in the fresh aftermath of an assault. I have to tamp down this demon within me, reign in the beast within me that wants to make her mine right now. I have to take care of her.

So that's what I do.

Chapter Eleven

Kylie

If I really believed in guardian angels, I would be convinced Liam is mine.

He's nothing but nice to me. He made sure I ate something that first night, and we got to know each other better.

He's thirty, and I found out he's the owner of Expon Communications. *The* Expon Communications that is only one of the biggest corporations in the entire world.

He's not overly involved in the business details of

it, though. He has someone else manage his business. He's just the owner who makes all the crazy big bucks.

He was in the marines. That explains his amazing physique. He only went into the marines to piss his father off. He never wanted to run the family business, but that didn't stop his father from leaving it to his only child when he died. Liam benefits from it money-wise, but he outsources all the work to someone else.

I was kind of embarrassed to tell him about my dinky little job at the library until he asked me all kinds of questions about it like he was genuinely interested. He didn't act like my job paled in comparison to his at all. On the contrary, he acted like it was fascinating to learn of all the mundane tasks I do every day.

He told me I could stay with him as long as I wanted to, that he certainly had more than enough space. I guess that *is* true. His mansion is huge, and he's the only one who lives here other than a few employees.

Still, manners were ingrained in me, and I never want to be a burden to anyone again like I know I was to my aunt and uncle. I accepted a room at Liam's place that first night, but I was determined to put on my big girl panties and go back to my apartment the next day.

When I got up the next morning after a surprisingly fitful night of sleep, I was all set to go to work and then return home. But when I voiced my plans, Liam was having none of it. He insisted I stay with him, assuring me I wasn't imposing and that I'd actually be doing him a favor because then he wouldn't worry about me. In fact, he'd been adamant about it, all but ordering me to let him take care of me.

It's been so long since I've had someone genuinely care about me enough to worry. I've not really had anyone care since my parents…

At his insistence, I called off work the first day after the assault. He had his driver take us to my apartment to get some clothes and other things I needed.

When I went back to work the next day, Liam insisted that his driver drive me. He rode with me too, and every day when his driver picks me up, he's there waiting in the limo too.

I still can't help feeling shy around him sometimes just because of his raw masculinity. Seriously, he's the kind of guy who walks into a room and his overpowering male presence just fills the whole atmosphere.

He asks me how my day is and hangs on my every

word. I know the details of my days at the library aren't really that fascinating, and I can't help wondering if he's just being nice or maybe he's just terribly lonely living all by himself in that huge mansion.

That doesn't make sense to me, though, because he's so hot. The man could have any woman he wants. I still can't believe he's not taken.

Still, I like Liam. He's my protector. He seems to like taking care of me, and I like letting him do it.

He has an in-home theater in his house where we eat popcorn and watch movies together when I get off work.

I love staying with him. I finally have someone to talk to, and I actually look forward to getting off work now. Liam's become my best friend—well, he's my *only* friend really.

But sometimes I still have those weird butterfly feelings when he looks at me so intensely. There's no doubt he's the most handsome man I've ever seen. He looks like a god chiseled from stone.

I kind of have a crush on him, but I know I'm just a girl he's helping because he's such a nice guy and maybe a bit lonely.

Sometimes I'll feel him staring at me, though, and when I look at him, he'll curse underneath his breath and leave the room for a few moments. Stuff like that's kind of confusing because I never know if I've done something wrong to piss him off or what. I don't know what I could have done, but I know that I don't ever want to irritate him. I want him to like me.

Sometimes when he calls me "honey," I imagine that he's attracted to me. Actually, sometimes I think he really might be attracted to me. I remember how his eyes looked that first day he brought me here when he was carrying me into his house and when I crossed my legs in the limo.

But then he's such a gentleman on a day-to-day basis that I think I imagined it all. I was pretty shook up after everything that happened with Mike. It's possible I was just hypersensitive after all that and just imagined Liam's reaction to me. It was probably just wishful thinking. Just because I've been fantasizing about him ever since that day we bumped into each other on the sidewalk doesn't mean that he's been doing the same. He probably never thought of me until he just so happened to be in the right place at the right time to rescue me from Mike. I shudder at the thought of Mike. I can still feel his harsh grip, but then I think of Liam's gentle one, and I'm calmed. He has that effect on me.

And Liam is such a hunk. He's a billionaire. What

would he want with a stupid little girl like me? It's enough that he was my friend, I tell myself.

Chapter Twelve

Liam

Having her living here with me is sweet torture. A thousand times a day I want to throw her over my shoulders, haul her up to my bedroom and ravish her.

If I ever had any doubt she's a virgin, I have none now. There's no way she's been touched before. She's so innocent, it borders on naiveté. She truly doesn't know I suffer beside her every night with a rock-hard erection while we watch a movie together.

She wears these cute little pajama sets with matching kitties on the tank tops and shorts. She has one with donuts on it. One with cherries. Fuck, I love that one. Hell, she's even got one with little strawberries on it. Every single fucking one is filled with innuendo about her pussy, but she doesn't fucking know that. All my adorable little butterfly knows is that she likes cute little pajamas with kitties, donuts, cherries and strawberries on them. She has no idea that all those things make me salivate thinking of how sweet her little virgin cunt would taste.

To top it all off, I know she doesn't wear a bra with them because sometimes I can see the outline of her nipples pebbling underneath the thin fabric. That makes me wonder if she has any panties on.

I'm killing myself here. I vowed I wouldn't jerk off again until it was for her. I'm so fucking wound tight just the smell of her shampoo as she flicks her hair over her shoulder is enough to make me feel like I'm going to go off like a cannon in my pants.

I don't know how much longer I can hold off, but I'm trying to give her space. I don't want to push her after what that asshole did to her. I want her to know she can trust me, that I really care about her. Christ, she equated me to a guardian angel. I can't take advantage of her when she places that kind of trust in me. That's why I'm doing everything within my power to be a gentleman.

I'm keeping my hands off her and just being

there for her, just taking care of her. I'll be her rock, anything she needs. I'll keep her safe and take her to work and pick her up from work.

She doesn't know it, but I still watch her every second of the day. When she thinks I've come back home after dropping her off at work, I'm really right outside so I can monitor everyone who goes in and out of the library.

I had one of my guys install hidden cameras inside of the library so I can watch her. I can't bear not having her within my sight at all times.

I sit in the limo all day and watch her on my monitor. The way her face gets all pensive when she's reading something thought-provoking. The way her brows knit prettily when she's reading something she doesn't understand. The way she smiles at the patrons, which makes my blood boil when it's a man. I know she's just being friendly and doing her job, but I'm jealous of her smiles. I don't want her smiling at any other motherfucker but me —so much so that I've yanked several of them by the collar into the alley beside the library to warn them away from her. I haven't seen any of them come back to the library. I'm killing the male patronage, and I frankly don't give a fuck. In fact, it'd suit me just fine if no man ever went in that fucking library where my little butterfly works ever again.

I have to leave the room more and more to get control of myself before I can come back and sit next to her. Every little thing she does is like gasoline on my flame. The way she licks her lips all the damn time. The way she bites and chews on them some-times when she's watching a movie. The way she runs a hand through her hair to push it out of her face only for the soft curls to cascade right back down. Even the way she pulls her legs up to the side and leans on the armrest, her toes with the pink nail polish peeking out at me. I've never had a foot fetish, but I want to lick her from head to toe, sucking on every precious inch of her.

I'm so infatuated with her I watch her sleep. I creep into her bedroom and sit there in the dark listening to her gentle little snores. I gaze down at her curls splayed out over her pillow, the way she always hugs one pillow up to her chest and throws her leg around it. This is how fucked up I am. I'm jealous of that damned pillow.

I pull her covers back up around her when she kicks them off and then shivers in her sleep—but not before I get a peek at the rounded globes of her ass cheeks peeking out from underneath those ridiculously short pajama shorts. I might as well strap my cock in a vice. That's what the sight does to me.

If she knew how many ways I've thought of fucking her, she'd run the other way. If she knew just how deep my obsession with her runs, it'd terrify her. If she knew I stalk her every second of the day…

Chapter Thirteen

Liam

We're sitting together per the usual watching a movie after I bring her home from the library. I can't tell you what the damn thing is about, though, because all I can do is flick my eyes over to her. I have a huge movie collection, and I always let her choose what we watch. Hell, I don't care what she puts on. The whole time I sit next to her, I breathe in her scent and study everything about her. The way her face reacts to everything she sees on the screen.

She's my movie. I could spend my entire life

watching her. Hell, that's all I've been doing since I first laid eyes on her. But I want to do so much more than watch her. I want to star alongside her, most specifically in her bed.

She's wearing my favorite pajama shorts tonight—the ones with the little cherries that drive me insane thinking about how I want to pop hers. She crosses her legs, and one of her little fuzzy slippers falls off her foot. She leans down to pick it up, and my eyes are riveted to the flash of skin I see at her back where her top hikes up as she bends over.

Hot damn. I see the top of her thong poking up from the back of her shorts as she bends over. Her thong is covered in cherries to match the shorts, and my cock instantly turns to an aching rod of steel in my pants as I hiss in my breath.

She puts the slipper back on her foot and then glances at me curiously, no doubt hearing my hiss.

"Are you okay?" she asks me, genuinely concerned for my welfare.

When I don't answer, she lays her tiny hand on my arm and then frowns when she feels how taut I am. "Liam?" she says my name questioningly, softly, leaning in closer to me.

Her scent surrounds me, and I can't believe she

can't see the huge tent in my pants, but she doesn't even look there. She's looking right into my eyes, and I can't take it. I want to throw her down on the seat and ravish her on the spot, tell her that no, I'm not okay, that I'll never be okay until I'm in that pussy, until I claim her fully as mine.

I jerk up roughly and leave the room before I do something we'll both regret, my breath coming raggedly. *Shit.* Why the fuck did I think I could be so near her without jacking off? I'm tempted to go into my room and relieve myself, but I know that won't stop the raging beast within me. I'll only be sated when I have *her*.

Speaking of her...I realize she's followed me when I smell her sweet scent close to me. My fists bunch at my sides as I hear her tentatively come up behind me.

"Kylie," I grind out. "Stay. Back." I can hardly breathe. I'm straining with the effort not to turn around and slam her against the wall and plunge into her over and over again. I'm like a fucking vampire who's fighting the scent of blood to keep from biting his victim. I'm a fucking druggie jonesing for a hit— only my drug of choice is *her*. It's everything about her.

One pump and I'd probably bust all inside her. My cock surges even more, threatening to tear clean through my pants as I think of coming deep inside her.

"Is it…is it something I've done?" she asks me worriedly. "Have I done something to upset you?"

I laugh jaggedly. "No, honey. You haven't done anything."

"Then what?" I hear the question in her sweet little voice, and her tiny hand reaches out to touch my arm again.

I detonate at the touch. My nerves are buzzing, my blood is boiling and her touch is like a match to dynamite. I turn around and grab her, pushing her up against the wall, lifting her until my throbbing cock is cradled right between the juncture of her thighs.

Her feet are hanging from the floor, and her mouth is a little "o" as her eyes finally widen in comprehension.

Her little tongue flashes out to lick her pink, full lips, and I can't take it anymore. I groan, my lips crashing down to claim hers.

Sweet. She tastes so fucking sweet. Like the littles cherries all over her shorts. I run my tongue along the seam of her lips, tasting her, prodding her to open for me, and she does with a little mewl, her arms going up around my neck.

I feel a surge of pride and victory as my tongue gains entry into the heaven of her mouth.

When her tongue moves softly against mine and I realize she's beginning to kiss me back, I can't stop the electricity that shoots to my engorged cock. I begin to rock my hips against her, dragging my thick dick up and down against her sweet little pussy, humping her through our clothes.

"Oh, fuck, honey," I whisper against her lips. "Do you know what I want to do to you?"

She gives a little gasp, and I make myself pull back enough to look at her. Her lips are wet and swollen from our kiss, her cheeks flushed, her eyes big. The sweet innocence shining in them reminds me she's a virgin, and I force myself to stop grinding against her, groaning with the effort. She deserves so much more than to have her virginity taken roughly up against a wall. I want to make her first time incredible. I want to savor every inch of her, have her so wet and shaking for me before I enter her slowly.

"Liam?" she says my name, and my cock twitches against her through my pants and her shorts. I see her eyes go wider at the sensation, and then she asks me, "Can I see it?"

I can't breath for a second. She's completely knocked the breath from me, my mind not quite believing what I just heard. The knowledge that she wants to see my cock about makes me lose control again. Her face colors even more when I don't immediately answer and she rushes to explain, "I've never seen a man before. You know, um, down there..." she trails off, and I groan.

"I'm sorry," she stammers. "I shouldn't have asked. I—"

I cut her off with a finger to her mouth and tell her, "No, honey. Don't ever be afraid to ask me anything. You can have any fucking thing you want. You understand me?" God, if she only knew just how true those words were. Anything. Anything within my power to give her.

She nods slowly, her big eyes shining up at me trustingly as I remove my finger from her sweet lips and reach down to unzip my pants. My stiff rod springs free, and her eyes get even bigger as she takes it in.

I'm so fucking horny with her gazing at me like that in wonder. My cock is purple, the head painfully swollen, precum beginning to leak from the tip. I try to choke back my groan, when she whispers, "It looks like it hurts."

"It does, honey," I tell her truthfully. "But there's a way to make it stop hurting."

"How?" she asks me, and I can tell she truly doesn't know. She's not just teasing me. *Fuck.*

"Do you want me to show you, honey?" My hand is already moving to my cock. God, I hope she says yes because I don't think I can stand another second without stroking it.

She nods, her eyes riveted between my legs, and that's all the encouragement I need. I close a fist around my shaft and begin to stroke it slowly from root to tip, groaning at the sensation. It's been too damn long since I've come, and knowing that the object of all my fantasies is standing right in front of me curiously watching me jerk off has my head swimming.

I will not fuck her right now, I tell myself, but I can come. I can come for her.

And I can make sure she knows what will happen when we have sex.

"This goes inside your pussy, honey," I tell her while rubbing my hand up and down my pole.

Her eyes widen at that knowledge, and she looks up at me dubiously. Holy fuck.

"When I put this inside your tight pussy, I'll stroke it in and out like this, sweet baby," I start to pump my hips forward into my hand, demonstrating to her.

She gasps, her eyes never leaving my cock. My eyes are riveted on her, imagining my cock balls deep inside her. I answer the question she doesn't ask but that I can tell is burning behind her eyes. "It'll fit, baby. I know it's big, but your sweet little pussy will stretch to take all of me. It'll hurt at first, but then it'll feel good. I promise you, little girl."

She clamps her thighs together trying to relieve the pressure there. I see her nipples pebble underneath her shirt, and I know she's turned on. God help me if that doesn't turn me on even more.

"Christ," I groan, my fist speeding up to fly over my cock, imaging it's her pussy gripping me.

"Then what?" she asks breathlessly.

"Then, I'll come and fill that pretty little pussy up with seed until it runs down your legs, baby."

She gasps at my filth, and I watch as she clamps her legs together even more. Fuck, she's horny and doesn't know what to do about it, but I sure as hell do. I want to eat her until her legs are shaking.

Her eyes are still riveted to my cock. She licks her lips, and that finishes me. I feel my balls seize up, and I know I'm there.

"Fuck, Kylie! Fuck, I'm coming. I'm coming for

you, baby!" I growl as I yank her shirt up just in time for the first rope of spend to release from me in a blast. She gasps and jumps as the first gush hits her skin, only making me come harder.

I double over her, holding myself up with one hand against the wall, my hips pumping into my fist, milking every last drop onto her stomach where it trickles down onto her cherry shorts.

My shoulders finally slump as I give my cock one last pump. Fuck, I don't think I've ever come so hard in my entire life. And Jesus, she looks so beautiful standing there covered in my spend.

I kiss her forehead, my precious girl. Then, I notice that she's still standing there, a shocked expression on her face. Shit, I probably scared her to death, jerking off on her like that like some kind of sick animal and talking filth to her.

And what kind of selfish bastard am I that I took care of myself without pleasuring her? She's standing there no doubt feeling confused and not knowing what to do.

"I'm just going to…I'm just going to go…" she waves near her stomach with a blush, unable to finish her sentence before practically sprinting from me toward her room.

Great. I close my eyes. Just fucking great. I've

frightened my little butterfly, and there she goes flitting away from me.

I move to go after her, but then I stop, deciding to give her space, praying I haven't ruined everything with my insatiable lust.

Chapter Fourteen

Kylie

Oh. My. God.

I keep replaying those moments when Liam orgasmed in my head. He looked so hot, and it turned me on so much to know that *I* made him like that. I can still feel how warm his cum was on my tummy. The way he screamed my name as he came…it makes me throb between my legs just thinking about it.

And his kiss…it was so much better than I could have ever imagined. I remember how it made my head spin and my knees weak. I've *never* been kissed like that. So passionately. Liam's kiss was filled with so much heat, it made moisture pool between my legs. How is that possible?

And the feeling of his huge manhood rubbing against my womanhood, the little electric currents it sent through my body when it rubbed over a certain spot. My face flushes just thinking about it.

After last night, something shifted between us. I've always been attracted to him, and I thought that maybe he was to me too, but now I *know*.

I wondered if things would be awkward between us after last night, but they're not. He rode with me to work like usual and made sure I have everything I need. Today has been like normal, only there seems to be a charge in the air between us. We haven't spoken of what happened last night, but his eyes seem to hold a promise of something to come when they light on me, and I find myself shivering in antic-ipation.

While I work, I find a book from the erotic romance section and begin reading through it, trying to learn more about the sexual act and what's expected.

I know it's crazy that I'm nineteen and don't know much of anything about sex, but my parents died before my mom ever got around to having "the talk" with me, and after their deaths, I was so focused on surviving, I didn't give much thought to dating or guys in general.

I read the book on and off between working, imaging the guy in the novel as Liam. I'm surprised when my sex throbs and grows wet as I read.

I blush at some of the things the couple does in the book, but I can't help wondering what it would be like to do them with Liam. Is *this* what he wants to do with me? Would it really feel as good as the author describes it in the book?

I don't know, but if it makes Liam happy, I want to do it. I want to be connected to him that way. I want him to want me that way.

Chapter Fifteen

Liam

Jesus. She's reading erotica. I'm sitting in the limo watching her over the monitor, and I zoom into what's she's reading, my cock growing hard to see her squirming in the chair in reaction to the scenes.

I've never seen her read anything like this. When she does read at work, she usually reads something educational or something about travel.

I've been worried I scared her last night, but I've obviously made her so curious that she's seeking out new literature. Fuck, doesn't she know I'll give her all the sexual education she needs?

We haven't spoken of what happened. I've tried to act normal, but every time I look at her, I'm filled with even more lust and love and hunger than before —if that's even possible.

Now, to see the evidence that she' obviously been affected by our encounter, that she's yearning to learn more…Christ…

My balls are so full and aching again it's like I never came yesterday. I've tried to give her space, gain her trust, show her that I truly care and that I'm not just trying to get in her pants.

I've waited as long as I can to claim her. I know I can't hold off much longer. As I sit and watch her squirm in her chair, the poor thing hot as hell and not knowing what to do about it, I think of all the ways to give her the relief she doesn't even know she needs.

Chapter Sixteen

Kylie

"Hi," I smile a little too cheerily as I get into the limo. My voice sounds odd even to my own ears. I can't help it, though. I finally know more about what Liam wants to do to me, and it has me feeling excited, nervous, and anxious all at once.

"How was work, honey?" Liam asks as I settle in across from him.

"It was good," I answer him a bit breathlessly. *Get ahold of yourself, Kylie.*

"Did you have time to do any reading today?" His eyes zero in on me intensely.

I lick my lips, and I see his eyes drop to them. "Yes," I answer him simply, but I can't keep the flush from riding up my neck.

"What'd you read about today?" he asks me casually, and I watch his eyes darken as that errant lock falls down onto his forehead. It's almost as if he *knows* the naughty stuff I was reading. But that's silly. There's no way he could know that, right?

My face colors even more, but I don't even consider lying to him. I don't ever want to lie to him. "Sex," I admit in a whisper.

"Sex," he repeats, and the way his voice lingers on the word makes heat pool between my legs. I instinctively press my legs together tighter, and his gaze drops to them.

"Why were you reading about sex, honey?" he asks me with a knowing glint in his eyes.

My own gaze drops to his crotch where I see that huge bulge in his pants. That bulge that was pressed right up against me yesterday.

I feel my nipples harden, and my breath catches as Liam doesn't wait for me to answer and gets on his knees in the floor of the limo, placing his hands gently on my legs, those gray eyes looking up at me intensely.

"Are you wet, Kylie?" he asks me as his hands stroke gently up and down the sides of my thighs.

My face heats, but again, I can't lie to him. "Yes," I whisper.

"I'll bet you've never come, have you, little girl?" He kisses my thigh and breathes in deeply before looking back up at me.

My heart is in my throat, and I can't speak, so I just shake my head.

"We need to fix that then, don't we?" he whispers, his hot breath fanning onto my thighs as he begins to kiss all over them, gently but firmly prying them apart with his hands.

I jump as he begins kissing the sensitive flesh on the insides of my thighs. "It's okay, baby," he tells me as he strokes up and down my legs like he's trying to calm a frightened animal.

He begins to alternate his kisses with licks as he works his way under my skirt, and that place between my legs begins to ache even more.

He pushes my skirt up to reveal my mound, that place that no one has ever seen before.

"Shit, Kylie," he groans as he strokes his hand over my panties, feeling the wetness through them. "You're fucking soaked for me, aren't you, baby?" I'd be embarrassed by the moisture there, but from what

I read earlier, I know wetness is normal, that it's a good thing. The way Liam groans with such hunger in his voice only affirms that for me.

"Liam," I whine, not knowing how to ask him what I need or exactly what it is I need. I just know that I need *something* and that he's the one who can give it to me.

"I know, honey. I know. That sweet little pussy aches, doesn't it? You need me to lick it, don't you?" He's stroking his thumb back and forth over something that's sending delicious tingles all through my body.

My breath hitches, and then in a move so sudden it causes me to gasp, he places his muscular arms under my legs and pulls me onto the edge of the seat, opening my legs wider, before yanking my panties to the side and smashing his mouth to my sex.

He licks up and down over my slit before tonguing his way through my folds. I throw my head back, my hands braced on the seat behind me. God, I can't believe how good his mouth feels. I never, never imagined it would feel like this.

He licks and sucks on me like I'm the best thing he's ever tasted, his hot breath fanning over my sensitive flesh as he talks to himself. "So sweet. Like fucking nectar. I'm going to eat you up, Kylie. Every last bit of you."

His words only serve to make me hotter, but then his tongue moves up to that sensitive little nub he was rubbing his huge manhood against last night, and I feel a pressure starting to begin within me as he pays it careful attention, licking and sucking on it.

It feels so good—too good. I can't sit still. I want to pull him closer and push him away at the same time. It's so intense I don't know what to do. My hands reach forward to sink into his hair. Oh my god, I can't take it.

"Liam, I can't—" I begin, panting, near tears, but he merely increases his suction, holding my legs open even wider.

"Yes. Yes, you can, baby," he urges me between licks. He pushes one finger slowly into me and then two, all while laving that sensitive little nub with his tongue.

I feel so full with the pressure of his fingers in me, and then his stormy eyes lock onto mine from between my legs. He raises his mouth just long enough to order me, "Come for me, baby. Let me feel that sweet little pussy convulsing around my fingers."

He latches back onto my nub, flicking harder, and then I feel that pressure building tighter and tighter until it finally bursts into a beautiful kaleidoscope of light. I can't stop the scream that rips from my throat as my legs shake. I fall back onto the seat as I feel muscles I didn't even know I had contracting.

Liam continues to lick and suck me, moaning, "Fuck, yes, baby. That little pussy fell right open for me, didn't it? Fuck, fuck, fuck." He pulls his fingers from my opening and licks them sensuously, his eyes trained on mine. "Taste like cherries, baby. So sweet."

He gives my womanhood one last parting kiss before he pulls my skirt back down and raises himself up to sit on the seat next to me, pulling me into his arms to settle me against his chest.

I feel the angry ridge of his erection pressing against my backside, and he groans at the contact, all the while stroking my hair and kissing my forehead.

I'm limp, my limbs shaky and spent. I couldn't move if I tried. I bury my head in his chest, and he pulls me closer.

"Mine. You're mine, Kylie. Do you understand me, honey?" I hear him whisper against the top of my head. "You're mine."

Yes, my soul speaks, *yours*, but I don't think he can hear me. I can't seem to find the strength to speak, so I sag into him and close my eyes.

Chapter Seventeen

Liam

Her first orgasm was beautiful. I almost came in my pants myself as she fell apart underneath my tongue, rewarding me with a flow of sweet honey.

I place another kiss upon her forehead as she sleeps in my arms, this precious, beautiful girl who I don't deserve. Not in a million years do I deserve her.

I'm selfish. I'm an asshole. I have no patience with anyone. Anyone but her. This sweet angel in my arms.

My cock is aching in my jeans, but I ignore it. There's no way I'm going to wake her.

When we finally get back to my place, I carry her up the stairs cradled in my arms, much like I did that first day I brought her here, only this time instead of staring up at me in a dazed sort of shock, she's sleeping trustingly.

I think my heart's about to burst through my chest as I carry her to the room she's been calling her own. I remove her little kitten heels and tuck her into bed. She immediately snuggles into the pillow with a soft sigh, never waking. I feel a rush of pride that I made her come so well she collapsed into a sated sleep afterward.

I settle into the chair in the corner of the room and keep watch over her as she sleeps. God help me, but I can't leave her just yet. I don't know if I'll ever be able to let her out of my sight again.

Chapter Eighteen

Kylie

I stretch languorously as I wake before I sit up groggily. I can tell from the moonlight streaming through the gauzy curtains over the French doors that it's still nighttime.

I look down to find myself still dressed in the clothes I wore to work and blush at the knowledge that I passed out on Liam and that he had to carry me up here and put me to bed.

"Oh my god, what must he think of me?" I groan to myself, covering my face with my hands.

"That you're the sexiest little creature I've ever

seen." His deep voice is suddenly right in my ear, and I gasp, looking up to find his stormy eyes level with mine. He sits on the bed next to me and begins to run his fingertips lightly up my leg.

"You've been watching me sleep?" I ask him. That's the only way he could be there, right?

"Does that bother you?" His gray eyes pierce mine, and that lock of dark hair falls over his forehead.

I finally give into that urge to push it back and lift my hand to do so.

"No," I answer him. I know I should probably find it creepy, but I'm honestly kind of flattered that he cares enough to watch me sleep.

That lock of hair is silky as I brush it back from his forehead, and he captures my hand with his own as I'm lowering it, turning his face into it and nuzzling it, planting an open kiss on my palm.

My breath hitches at the sensation, and his eyes capture mine as he begins to drop kisses along my fingers, the inside of my wrist, and then up the inside of my arm. He reaches my neck, where he finally growls and then begins laving it with his tongue as his arms go around me to pull my chest flush against his.

My arms go around his neck instinctively, pulling

him closer, and a whimper escapes me. I feel so small against him, and for some reason that excites me.

He groans, his hands moving up to angle my head toward him, and he kisses me hotly. The heat of his kiss goes straight to my sex, moisture immediately pooling there.

He drags me onto his lap, and I feel the length of his erection settle between my thighs as he wraps my legs around him. The next thing I know, his hands are everywhere, running over my legs, gripping my backside and then finally pushing my shirt up and over my head.

"Jesus, Kylie," he croaks as he takes in my white, lacy bra. He begins to kiss the exposed parts of my breasts, and I shiver. His fingers adeptly unhook my bra, and I feel the rush of air hit them as they're bared to his hungry eyes, my nipples instantly pebbling.

He groans and then his tongue reaches out to flick one.

It's like a hot wire is running from my nipple to my sex, for I feel the sensation register down *there*, and I gasp in surprise.

He grins up at me wickedly, as if he knows exactly what I just felt. He circles his tongue around the hard nub again before latching on and sucking. I can't help throwing my head back and arching my breasts up to him. An offering he doesn't hesitate to accept. He feasts on my orbs before tearing his mouth from them long enough to come back up and capture my mouth again.

My sex is so wet, and I feel his manhood straining against it. I feel it pulsing through our clothes, and I can't stop my hand from moving down to touch it.

He sucks in a sharp hiss at the contact and stills my hand, lifting my chin to look him straight in the eyes. The storm within them is raging with lust, and my stomach gives a little flutter knowing that it's for me.

"Kylie," his voice comes out strangled, and the muscles of his arms are bunched as if he's physically restraining himself. It gives me such a rush of power to know that *I* put him on the brink of losing control like this. "Are you sure you want this, baby?" he asks me seriously. "Because once I start, I don't think I'm going to be able to stop. You're going to be mine in every way. Do you understand what I'm saying to you, sweet girl?" He growls that last bit, cupping my face with his hand, stroking his thumb over my lips.

I don't know what causes me to do it. I'm just letting my instincts lead. I part my lips and take his thumb into my mouth, sucking on it.

He sucks another sharp breath in, hissing, "Goddammit, Kylie. If your answer isn't yes, you'd better stop right the fuck now."

His curses turn me on even more, and I look directly into his eyes as I answer, "Yes, I want this."

Liam flips me onto my back so fast I hardly have time to register what's happened. And then suddenly he's kissing me all over, licking, sucking, and nipping every bit of my flesh. His hands are tugging down my skirt and panties until I'm completely bare before him.

He pulls his own shirt off and then sits up to look down at me, whispering, "Jesus, so fucking perfect."

In a moment of shyness, I start to cover myself, but he pins my hands up, threading his fingers through mine. "Never hide yourself from me, baby," his lips whisper against mine before kissing me deeply, his tongue mating with mine in a sensual twist, dipping in and out of my mouth in a foreshadow of what our bodies are soon going to be doing.

His hands release mine to skim over my skin, down my tummy, and to that apex of my thighs where he rubs between my legs, groaning at the moisture he finds there. "You're so fucking wet for me, baby. You need my cock, don't you, honey?"

I simply nod as he raises his hips closer to me and

places my hands on his erection. "If you want this, Kylie, you let it free."

I stare at the huge bulge in his pants, and then with shaking fingers, I begin to unzip him. He groans loudly as his heavy sex springs free and slaps onto my belly. My eyes widen at how hard yet soft it is, and my fingers reach down to skim the tip where liquid oozes from the tip.

I don't know why I do it, but I gather the liquid on my fingertip and then raise it to my lips to taste it. It's salty and creamy at once.

That seems to put him over the edge because his eyes darken, and he growls, "Holy fuck, Kylie. Do you know what you've just unleashed? Do you, baby?" He tears his pants the rest of the way from his body before he settles down on top of me, the thick head of his member prodding the opening of my center.

One of his hands holds himself up to keep from putting his full weight on me while the other reaches down between us to guide himself as he starts to push ever so slowly into me.

"Liam," I can't stop the whine that leaves my lips at the pressure. I wiggle, trying to get more comfortable as he continues to push slowly until he reaches a barrier. He has a few inches in, but I see how far he still has to go and start doubting whether it's all going to fit.

"Sshhh, it's okay's, baby." He's stroking the sides of my face, my hair, petting me, soothing me. I can see the genuine anguish on his face at my discomfort, but it's mixed with the lust of his desire. "It's going to hurt a little bit, but then I'm going to make it feel better. I promise." He bends down to take my nipple into his mouth, effectively distracting me, although I still feel his pressure between my legs. I begin to relax against him, the sensations he's causing at my breast traveling down between my legs in tingles that are throbbing in time with the pulses of his hardness within me.

Suddenly, he surges into me in a rush, and I can't stop my cry as a sharp pain rips through me. His moan mingles with my cry, and my fingers dig into his shoulders. His breathing is heavy against my lips as he tells me, "I'm sorry, honey. I'm sorry for hurting you. Take some time to get used to me."

His arms and neck are taut with his effort not to move as he gives me time to adjust. I'm clinging to him, almost sobbing while he keeps whispering words of apology to me over and over again, but then the pain begins to subside and is replaced by a pressure that's throbbing and almost unbearable. I wiggle a bit underneath him, trying to relieve it. A groan tears from his throat, and I see the muscles in his abdomen roll.

"Christ, Kylie. I'm not going to be able to hold still much longer, baby."

I lift my hips a little, testing the movement, and I feel his huge erection slide within me, sending a ripple of sensation inside the walls of my sex. "Oh," I moan in surprise.

He groans like a man tortured, and then his mouth crashes down upon mine. "Can't fucking do it," he whispers against my lips. "Got to move, baby. That thing is gripping me too tight."

"Do it," I give him my permission, and that's all he needs. He pulls out of me some and then plunges back in, groaning again. God, his groans of pleasure are sexy as hell, and I can't help answering with a moan of my own.

He keeps plunging in and out, pulling more of his hardness out each time until he's finally plunging completely in and out of me, his eyes looking down at me wildly.

He picks up speed, his thrusts getting faster and harder, and I feel his stiff rod hitting this delicious spot inside me. I wrap my legs around his waist, and then he gathers me into his arms, angling himself so his thick erection is not only hitting that spot deep inside me, but the length of it is also rubbing along that little nub on the outside that he licked and sucked earlier.

"Yes," he hisses as my arms go around his neck. "Hold on to me baby. I got you. I got you. You're mine, aren't you, honey?" He's speaking through gritted teeth, his breath rasping in my ear, and that pressure is building within me. "Mine," he growls, his eyes looking into my mine intensely, so intensely I don't think I can stand it. His eyes are wild with possession, and god, it turns me on to see it. "You're fucking, mine, Kylie. Only mine," he tells me as he continues to claim me. "Tell me you're mine," his eyes order me with an unbridled desperation like he'll die if I don't confirm it.

"Yours," I gasp.

"Fucking right, baby," his eyes light with victory. "I'm the only one who's ever going to be inside you like this. Do you understand me? No one else will ever have you like this."

I'm nodding, agreeing with him, Yes, yes, only him. Only him.

The inside of my pussy is tingling where he's stroking it, and I'm gasping, reaching, for something.

"Liam," I beg, clawing at his back, though what I'm begging for I'm not quite sure.

"Yes, baby. You say my name when you come. Scream it for me." He's pumping into me furiously now, his balls slapping against my butt. I feel his erection growing impossibly longer and larger within me. He's harder than steel, and I feel his tip swelling within me, rubbing that glorious little spot, kissing it over and over again.

"Not gonna last," he pants, licking his thumb and then moving it down to rub the nub on my mound.

"Oh, god!" I arch up at the contact and then I burst around him, screaming his name, "Liam!"

"Fuck! Fuck, yes!" he growls. "That fucking pussy is falling open all around me." I feel myself clenching and convulsing in a pleasure so intense I see stars, and then Liam is howling my name, and I feel warm liquid shooting deep within me, coating my insides with his hot seed.

He keeps pumping, his breaths coming out hoarsely as he twitches and spasms within me until I feel his hot sperm running down my thighs.

I'm stunned, not only by the floaty, tingling sensations still coursing through my body, making my limbs numb but also at the sheer volume of fluid Liam sprayed into me. It's warm inside me, and I feel full and wanted.

He falls onto his side without releasing me and gathers me into his arms, planting kisses all over my face. "You're mine, baby," he tells me. "Mine. I'm never going to let you go."

And I don't want him to.

Chapter Nineteen

Liam

After Kylie falls asleep in my arms in the aftermath of our lovemaking, I take her to the master bedroom and lay her down on my bed. She's sleeping with me from now on. She's mine. She agreed to it, screaming my name and quaking beneath me. Giving herself to me in every way.

My obsession is driven home with the taking of her virginity. I've never received a sweeter gift. Instead of slaking my lust, it only heightens it. Instead of curbing my obsession, it only amplifies it.

I don't know how I'm going to be able to cope

with it. I need her every second of the day. I want to lock her up here with me and never let her leave, but I know I can't do that. She'll grow to resent me if I keep her a prisoner.

She tosses in her sleep, mumbling my name, and my heart swells in pride. Me. It's me she dreams of. My name she calls in the middle of the night.

"I'm here, baby," I whisper against her ear before taking her lips, gently kissing her awake. She's so soft, fresh from sleep, and she melts in my arms willingly.

Her arms wind around my neck, pulling me closer. I know I should wait to take again. Her body needs to recuperate, but God knows I can't resist her when she's pulling me to her, so I take her gently, the way she should have been taken her first time, stroking in and out of her ever so slowly, kissing her shoulders, her neck, every inch of her I can find.

Her soft moans are music to my ears. The pressure builds between us slowly until it crashes around us in waves. I'm sweating as I hold off my own release until I feel her clench around me. Then I let go, jumping into that pool of pleasure with her. There's nothing like this sensation of our bodies clenching and releasing together, her sweet cunt milking every last drop from me.

"I love you, Kylie," I confess to her in the heat of our passion.

She stiffens beneath me, and I think I've spoken too soon, scared her away, but then I hear her sweet little voice answering the words I'd give my life to hear, "I love you too, Liam."

And I can't help it. I take her again.

Chapter Twenty

Kylie

Liam made love to me all night. Slow, hard, fast, over and over again, raining words of love, devotion and filth upon me in turns. And I loved every moment of it. After each session, he held me close in his arms as if he never wanted to let me go. He couldn't stop touching me. He made me feel loved and cherished in a way I never have.

So when morning comes, and I try to wiggle out of his arms to get ready for work, I'm not entirely surprised when he pulls me close to him again, breathing in the scent of my hair and kissing my neck.

"Where you going, baby?" he asks in between licks and nibbles that send my toes curling.

"I've got to get ready for work, Liam," I say, gently pushing him away, knowing that if he continues on this path, I'll never make it on time.

He props up on an elbow, that errant lock of hair falling down on his forehead, his beautiful mouth frowning down at me. "You know you don't have to work, baby. I can take care of you."

I feel a little ball of warmth in the pit of my stomach that he wants to take care of me, but I need to maintain some sense of responsibility. I can't lay here all day, every day with him. Can I?

I sit up, pulling the sheet with me to keep my breasts covered. "I know, but I like my job, Liam. It might not pay much, but I truly enjoy it, and it's just something that I need to do."

He continues to frown, both at my words and at me holding the sheet up over me. He unlatches my fingers from it, and it slips from my grasp. The rush of air on my exposed breasts makes my nipples instantly harden, and he eyes them hungrily. "What did I say about never hiding from me? Hmm?"

His head begins to lower, but before he can take

my nipple into his mouth, I jump out of bed, grab-bing the sheet with a giggle and spinning to wrap it around me before I dash off down the hall to go get dressed.

I hear his frustrated groan drifting from his bedroom, and I'm tempted to give in and call in sick today.

But, no. I can't do that. It wouldn't be right to shirk my responsibilities like that. No matter how much I may want to.

Chapter Twenty-One

Liam

I don't know why she insists on working. I need her in my arms. My arms physically ache to hold her. She's like a phantom limb. I can feel her even though she's not here.

My cock stiffens when I think of how she fell apart, quivering underneath me while I fucked her brains out, her lips swollen, her hair mussed. She's a beautiful fucking angel, and I'm the depraved demon stealing her purity, but I can't help myself. I'd do it all over again. And I will. As soon as I get her ass back in my arms.

I rub a hand over my face. Why does she have to be so stubborn? Why can't she just accept what I want to give her?

I should be grateful that she's obviously not sleeping with me because of my money. Not like so many other women.

No, she's hellbent on leaving me every day to go to work—despite the fact that she knows I have more than enough money to give her the world. She's fiercely independent in that respect. It both frustrates and endears her to me to no end. And I don't know if I'll be able to take it.

It was somewhat more bearable before, watching her from the monitor, but that was before she let me inside her.

I want to stalk in there, throw her over my shoulder, and carry her home with me like an ogre. I don't necessarily want to lock her up and take away her freedom, but I want her with me at all times.

How am I going to deal with her working? Other men looking at her? Her smiling at them? I want to roar just at the thought. Hell, I could hardly deal with it before.

She's mine now. My impossible obsession somehow got worse.

This time without her is hell. I'm staring at the

clock, willing it to move faster. I'm glaring out the window of the limo at the sun, cursing it to go down already.

I make a decision here and now.

She'd better enjoy working today because it's the last day she's ever going to work in that library.

Chapter Twenty-Two

Kylie

Works seems to drag. I'm counting the minutes until I get off and get to be with Liam again. More than once today, I've thought that I should have taken him up on his offer to stay home with him. It's not like I truly need my job if I'm going to be his. I get a delicious shiver up my spine just thinking of how possessive he is and the look in his eyes when he tells me I'm his.

He never lets me pay for anything anyway. He's a freaking billionaire. He doesn't want for anything.

Still, it's the point of the matter, isn't it? I need to

do something for myself. He's already done so much for me. It wouldn't be right for me to just let him do everything. Or that's what I keep telling myself anyway.

I never text while I'm at work, and I don't really have anyone to text anyway, so that's why I start when I hear my phone buzz in my purse.

I pull it out to find a text from Liam.

I miss you, baby.

I melt at his words.

I smile as I text him back.

I miss you too.

I watch the three dots that let me know he's texting me back dance up and down, and then I get a new text from him that makes my heart trip in my chest.

I'm going to ravish you as soon as you step foot in this limo.

*In this limo…*He writes as if he's already in the limo. I glance at the clock. He's probably already on his way to pick me up. It's less than thirty minutes until the library closes, after all.

I press my thighs together, feeling that little nub that Liam told me was my clit throbbing. He's taught me so many things…

I hear another buzz and look down at my phone again.

Are you wet, baby?

My face flushes as I look around ridiculously as if anyone knows what my texts say. No one's around. All the patrons are either browsing the shelves or tucked away behind desks reading or on computers.

Maybe, I type back with shaking fingers.

Fuck, Kylie. I can't wait to get in that sweet pussy.

Gotta go, I text back quickly as a patron walks up.

I'm busy for the rest of the time I'm there, checking books out and answering questions, but my stomach is full of butterflies every time I look at the clock and see the minute hand ticking closer to time for me to leave.

Finally, the time to leave arrives, and I'm so eager to get back to Liam that I'm basically sprinting down the stairs to the limo. I trip over the last stair in my haste, but one of the patrons who checked out a book earlier steadies me.

"Whoa, careful there, little—"

Suddenly, he's jerked back and a fist smashes into his face. I gape in horror as I see Liam's face snarling, contorted with rage, his stormy eyes rolling with thunder.

"Don't. Fucking. Touch. Her." He punctuates each word with a punch.

"Liam!" I grab hold of his arm to keep him from beating the man to a pulp.

He instantly calms at my touch, but his eyes still scream murder.

"Come on," he orders me, wrapping his arm around my shoulders and ushering me toward the limo. He towers behind me as I step down into it, and then he follows right behind me, pulling me roughly against his chest, rapping the glass with his knuckles to let the driver know it's time to move.

I feel his heart beating a mile a minute, and then his hands are in my hair tipping my face up to him so he can claim my mouth.

He kisses me like a man starved, and I fall into him. All the words of reproach that were on my lips melt away in the heat of his kiss.

"Nobody touches you, baby. You understand me? No one. You're mine," he growls, nipping and licking at my lips.

I know his possession should probably be frightening, but it's intoxicating instead. I'm drunk on his affection, and I want another shot.

"Say it," he commands, moving to suck on my neck, sending shivers up and down my spine.

"I'm yours."

"Goddammit," he heaves as he pushes my skirt up and pulls my panties to the side, pulling me onto his lap. He holds me hovered there as he adeptly unzips his pants, freeing his cock like a monster from a cage. Then he positions himself at my entrance before thrusting up with his hips and pulling me down at the same time, going straight to my core.

I scream at the penetration, my flesh convulsing around him immediately, the sensation of his head kissing my cervix causing me to come immediately.

"Look at you coming for me already, baby. Hot damn, my sweet little librarian. Wearing these sexy little skirts to work every day just begging to get fucked by my cock, aren't you?"

He pumps into me viciously. I'm holding onto his shoulders for dear life, my head bobbing up and down.

"Aren't you? Answer me, Kylie!" His voice quips over my skin like a whip, and I couldn't disobey if I wanted to.

"Yes!" I scream.

"Yes, what?" His stormy eyes are flashing lightning.

"I'm begging to be fucked by your cock," I sob as another orgasm wracks my frame.

"Fuck yes, baby. Fuck," he's hammering up into me roughly, and I feel him growing harder inside me, the head of his cock swelling.

"Fuuuck." He gasps the word out as I feel him explode inside me, his spend spraying deep within me. Once again, he fills me to the brim until hot seed rolls out of my pussy, dripping down onto his balls, both of us spent and clinging to each in the aftermath of our passion.

Dear god, is it like this for everyone? Something tells me that it's not. That Liam and I are special.

While still sitting in Liam's lap, I suddenly notice a screen propped up in the corner of the seat. It looks like a laptop screen yet smaller.

I peer at it for a moment before I realize what I'm seeing. "Oh my god." My hand flies up to cover my mouth as I realize it's different angles of the library—more specifically where I sit while at work.

I look back to find Liam studying me carefully.

I start to move off him, but his hands tighten on my waist possessively.

"You've been watching me," I accuse him.

"Yes." He doesn't try to hide it, his face impassive.

"For how long?" I ask him, my voice flat.

He doesn't say anything for a long moment, and when he does speak, he doesn't answer me.

"Kylie, I love you." His eyes are trained on mine, burning into me with heat. "You're my world."

"How long?" I repeat, my voice becoming shriller as everything suddenly clicks, and I stare down at him, my mouth gaping. "That day that he tried—that's how you were able to—that's why you were there." My head is spinning trying to process it all. He's been watching me. He was watching me before we actually met. The tingles up my spine. Those hadn't been imagined. It's because I felt him. I felt I was being watched.

"Ever since that day you ran into me, Kylie, I just couldn't get you out of my head. I had to know more about you. I had to find out who you were."

"So you stalked me?" I ask incredulously.

I begin to shake as the enormity of his words begin to wash over me. He's been watching me all this time. He found out stuff about me. What all did he already know about me?

He'd stalked me. That was creepy, right? I was supposed to be angry. This is unacceptable. It's inappropriate. He's invaded my privacy. He's insane. He's mad. He's dangerous. This isn't right.

But...

But his eyes are looking at me so intensely. He has

no shame in them. If anything, there's only a fierce determination.

"Let me go, Liam," I tell him, pushing against his chest, but he doesn't relax his grip on my waist.

Instead, he pulls me closer, stilling me with his gaze. "Never. I can't ever let you go, baby. I told you last night once I claimed you, you would be mine forever."

His eyes only seem to intensify as he shakes his head, his voice coming out in a rasp on his next confession. "God help me, Kylie. Don't you see? I *can't*. I can't let you go. It would be the death of me. I can't survive without you in my life."

He looks down for just a moment before looking back up and capturing my eyes with his once again, but instead of seeing a raging storm there, this time I see rain, a deep sadness. The sight twists my heart, and it humbles me that this big, strong man could be reduced to this because of *me*.

"I know it's wrong, honey, but I can't breathe if I don't watch you every second of the day. You're my everything." He pulls in a shuddering breath before continuing, "Maybe I'm too obsessive, but I can't help it. I swear to you I'd never harm a hair on your head. All I want to do is take care of you, protect you from everything. I'll give you anything you want.

But I *need* you completely. I need your continual presence in my life. I'm not one of the those guys who can go halfway. It's got to be everything for me."

His eyes darken, and his voice comes out strained. "I can't stand the thought—let alone the sight—of another man's hands on you."

His hands tighten around my waist possessively with that statement.

"Liam, you have to let me go," I try to repeat more firmly, but my voice sounds shaky to my own ears."

Liam studies me knowingly, as if he knows the conflict within me. Part of me is flattered that he wants me that much. Another part is outraged at the invasion of my privacy.

"If," he begins, his lips coming to hover right above mine, his breath hot against them, "you can honestly tell me you don't love me, that your pussy isn't wet and throbbing for me right this second," he pauses, capturing my eyes with his again, the smoke churning within them, "I'll let you go."

I don't say anything, a lump in my throat. I could lie to him. My mind tells me I should, but my heart screams 'no.' No, I should never lie to him. I can't lie to him. I don't want to lie to him. I want to be possessed by him. I want his crazy, possessive, insane love. "I…" I begin, but I can't finish.

"You what, Kylie?" His eyes are smoldering at me, and I can't think straight. God, I've been alone for so long—since my parents died, and I've never had a man make me feel safe the way Liam does, love me the way he does.

I look into the stormy depths of his eyes and know without a shadow of a doubt that he would do anything for me. He'd kill for me. He'd die for me. He loves me with a love so intense it's obsessive but… would I really want it any other way?

"I love you," I finally confess in a sob, throwing my arms around his neck and melting into him.

"My love," he kisses me passionately. "My life," he kisses me again. I feel his hardness pressing into my tummy insistently, and his hands cup my buttocks as he lifts me once again. "Mine," he bites my neck as he impales me on him, our bodies, hearts, minds, and souls joining together as one.

Two Years Later

Liam

My breath seizes as I watch her sitting in the library. My wife.

The thought that she's mine never ceases to send a rush of lust through me. I thank God every day that my little butterfly bumped into me that day on the street.

By some miracle, she loves me, all of me, even the possessive parts of me that obsess over her. She's patient with all of me and puts up with my demanding nature.

She doesn't work anymore. I finally convinced her to stay here with me and let me spoil her.

I bought a private jet so I can take her all over the world and show her all the sights she always read about and never thought she'd get to see. Nothing gives me more pleasure than making her happy.

We decided not to have any children. Thank God, she'd never been the type of girl who'd dreamed of having them because bastard that I am, I don't think I could share her even with our own child. I'm so fucking twisted for her like that.

But she loves it. I know she does.

She knows I have to have her in my sight at all times, and thank God, she's okay with that. I'm such a psycho over her I had cameras installed in every room of the fucking house just so I can find her at a moment's notice.

She knows I'm always watching, and she's started using it to her advantage, the little minx. She knows exactly where the cameras are.

Right now she's wearing a filmy red dress that should be against the law. I watch her as she closes the book she's reading and lays it on the table before her.

My lips quirk up. Tired of reading, my love? Need something else?

She leans back on the tufted chaise lounge and spreads her legs, my cock twitching in response. I reach down to readjust it.

Holy fuck, she's not wearing any panties, the naughty girl. Her fingers slip down to stroke herself.

I'm instantly hard and curse under my breath. Fuck, she knows what's she doing.

I watch for a few more moments as she rubs her clit sensuously and then finally dips her finger into her wet hole.

Jesus Christ, I can see it glistening over the camera.

I rub my erection with an open palm, continuing to watch her pleasure herself until she looks up right into the camera.

That's my cue. Her eyes are summoning me, and I jump to obey, striding quickly down the halls with my hard staff tenting my pants and leading the way.

She rises to her knees when I enter, sucking her own juices from her fingers, her eyes locking onto mine mischievously. Christ, how can she look so innocent and yet so sinful at the same time?

I walk up to her, pulling my cock from my pants

as I go. "I'll give you something to suck on if you're hungry, little girl."

Her mouth opens readily, and I feed my cock to her. She moans as she takes me in, deep throating me like a champ, her blue eyes shining up at me all the while.

The way her tongue is swirling around my tip and her cheeks are caving in a sweet suction has my balls churning. I slip my length from her mouth, knowing that if I don't, I won't last long enough to fuck her.

She whimpers at the loss, and I shush her reassuring, "Don't cry, baby. I'm going to give it back to you."

I flatten her to the couch, hiking her dress up to give me a full view of her pussy.

I rub the head of my cock up and down her pussy, teasing her clit. She closes her eyes and lifts her hips, her body begging for me.

Oh yes, my sweet little girl loves this dick, and I love nothing more than to give it to her.

I continue to tease her, rubbing my thick head back and forth along her slit, her slick juices mixing with the precum that leaks from my tip.

"Liam," she begins to beg my name, and I break, a rope of precum shooting onto the top of her pussy.

I can never hold back when she begs for my cock. Hell, what man could?

I shove inside her in one deep thrust, pushing until I'm fully seated in her, my aching balls resting against her ass.

She's so fucking little. I don't know how she takes it all. I must be all the way up in her stomach.

She cries out and arches her back like a kitten arching into its master.

"See? I told you I'd give it back to you, baby," I soothe her as I stroke her languidly, petting my hands along her hair, over her throat and down her arms. Goosebumps breaks out on her skin, and her rosy little nipples harden.

I bend over and tease one with my tongue, picking up the pace of my strokes until I'm thrusting so deep in her the chaise is bouncing as it scoots across the floor.

She screams as she reaches her orgasm, the muscles of her pussy clenching violently around me as I saw in and out of her.

It never fails to fill me with a sense of pride when I push her over the edge like that.

God, my wife is so sexy coming on my dick. It's enough to push me over the brink too, and I roar my own release as I feel the rush of come jet up my stalk and burst through the head of my cock deep into her womb.

My own orgasm is so intense I struggle to catch my breath, and my eyes feel like they're going to roll back in my head. I collapse on top of her, kissing her lips deeply as she purrs her love in my ear. This beautiful little butterfly that flitted into my life, obsessing me until my senses are filled with nothing but her.

Mine. Forever mine.

Connect With Emma!

Visit Emma's website to get a FREE book you can't get anywhere else: www.authoremmabray.com.

www.ingramcontent.com/pod-product-compliance
Lightning Source LLC
Chambersburg PA
CBHW031741150726
47989CB00006B/2548